Rookie
Read-About® Science

Around and Around

By Patricia J. Murphy

Consultants
Martha Walsh, Reading Specialist

Jan Jenner, Ph.D.

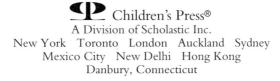

Children's Press®
A Division of Scholastic Inc.
New York   Toronto   London   Auckland   Sydney
Mexico City   New Delhi   Hong Kong
Danbury, Connecticut

Designer: Herman Adler Design
Photo Researcher: Caroline Anderson
The photo on the cover shows a child spinning on a whirl on the beach.

Library of Congress Cataloging-in-Publication Data

Murphy, Patricia J
    Around and around/ by Patricia J. Murphy.
      p.cm.—(Rookie read-about science)
    Includes index.
    Summary: A simple introduction to circular movement and the forces
that affect it.
    ISBN 0-516-22550-2 (lib. bdg.)   0-516-26863-5 (pbk.)
    1. Rotational motion—Juvenile literature. [1. Rotational motion.] I.
Title. II. Series.
  QC133.5 .M85 2002
  531'.34—dc21

                    2001002685

Everywhere you look,
things move around you.

Some things move around
and around, or in a circle.

Carnival rides move around and around high in the sky.

Ballerinas dance in circles
on stage.

The Earth spins around
in space.

The moon makes a circle
around the Earth every
twenty-eight days.

You move around and around, too.

When you do somersaults, you are moving around and around!

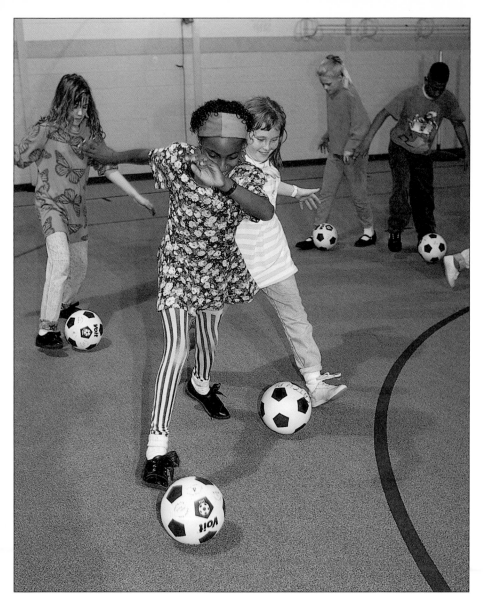

How do things move
this way?

Gravity (GRAV-uh-tee)
is the force that pulls all
objects toward the Earth.

But objects need another
force, or a push, to start
or stop moving.

YOU are the force that stirs
ingredients to make cookies.

YOU turn the water faucet
on to wash your hands.

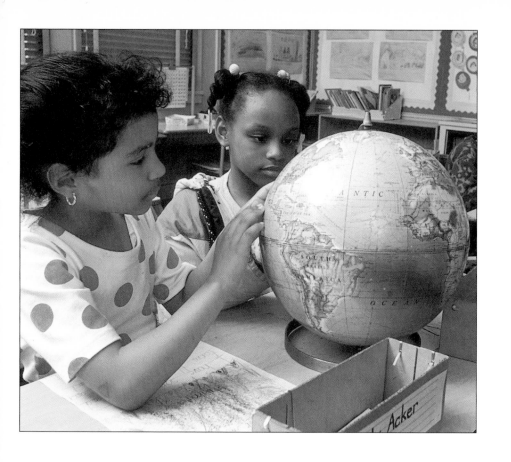

YOU spin the globe in
your classroom to find the
countries of the world.

YOU turn the doorknob to come in and out of a room.

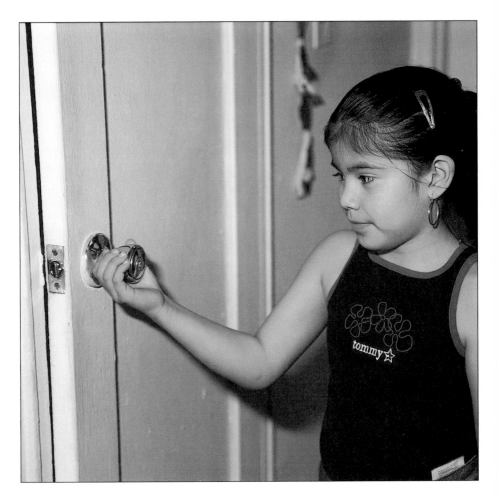

YOU push the pedals on your bike. This makes the wheels go around.

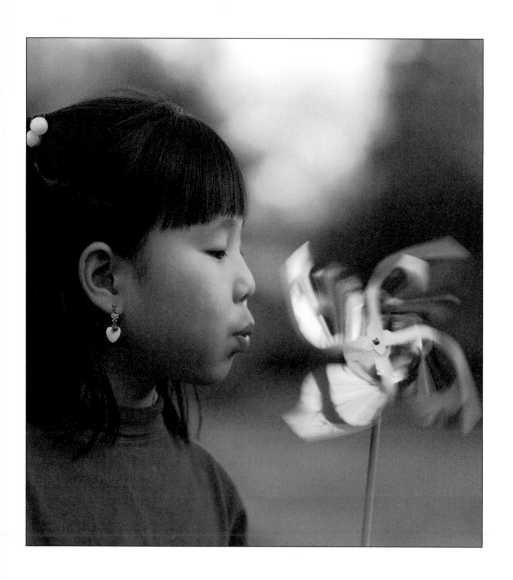

Wind is the force that blows pinwheels around and around. Once the force stops, the object stops moving.

What happens to a pinwheel when the wind stops blowing?

Centrifugal (sen-TRIF-yuh-guhl) force keeps an object traveling around and around in a circle.

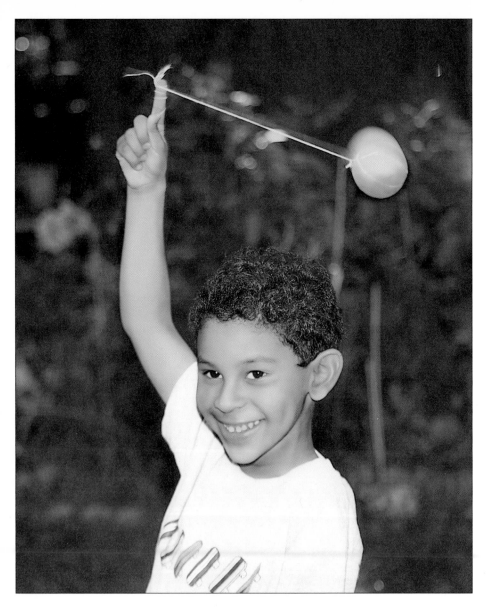

You can feel this force if you tie a string to a ball and spin it above your head. Be careful!

When you stop spinning, the ball will fall in a straight line.

We use centrifugal force with everyday things.

Washing machines and dryers use it. Can you think of any others?

Everywhere you look,
things move around you.

Words You Know

ballerinas

carnival ride

centrifugal force

circle

pinwheel

somersault

31

Index

About the Author

Patricia J. Murphy lives in Northbrook, IL, where she writes children's books. She also writes for magazines, corporations, and museums. Patricia loves to travel around and around the world—especially to Ireland.

Photo Credits

Photographs © 2002: Corbis-Bettmann/Richard Cummins: 29; NASA: 8; Photo Researchers, NY/John Foster: 9; PhotoEdit: 11, 31 bottom right (Robert Brenner), 27 (Tony Freeman), 20, 31 bottom left (Richard Hutchings), 16, 23, 30 bottom right (Michael Newman), 14 (David Young-Wolff); Rigoberto Quinteros: 4, 6, 15, 17, 24, 30 bottom left, 31 top; Superstock, Inc.: 3; The Image Works: 12, 19 (Bob Daemmrich), cover (Peter Hvizdak), 7, 30 top (Kent Meireis).